Look For Me When You Know What You Want

MÓNICA BENÍTEZ

Chapter 1

Marina walks down the street almost wanting to run. She doesn't like Christmas, this will be the third one since Elisa left her the day before Christmas Eve with a cold message on her cell phone. It was a joke she thought, a prank that came before the hour, but it was as real as the fact that she never saw her again after almost three years of dating. She didn't have an explanation, she doesn't know if she did something wrong or if there was someone else. The uncertainty haunted her for months, until one day she simply stopped caring.

The cold is soaking into her bones, and she rubs her arms as she keeps walking and window shopping this way and that without deciding on anything. She hates it when that happens. She also hates being so indecisive and leaving everything for last. Her brother has been insisting that she have dinner with them at the family's house in a mountain village for over a month, but Marina, although grateful, didn't think it was a very good idea, considering that her three nephews scream like pigs all day long, and she is a woman who likes calm. So why did she decide to go? Because she's sick of hearing her friend Lola tell her she's a sourpuss. She has also invited her to her house, but if she has to choose between the pigs and the lewd and uncomfortable looks that her friend's perverted boyfriend gives when Lola doesn't notice, she'll take the former.

Maybe someday she'll get up the courage to explain to her friend that she's living with a pervert, but for now she stands by and waits for her to open her eyes and realize it. Perverts and pigs, she thinks and laughs to herself in the street as she realizes she must look like a crazy person. It's starting to sleet and that makes her even more nervous. It's almost eight o'clock in the evening, the stores are about to close, and she still hasn't found the gift for her brother.

"Fuck it" she says, walking into a men's clothing store.

She has just decided to buy him a tie, that never fails because her brother graduated in law, it seems that in addition to a degree, he was also given an order that obliged him to always dress in a suit.

Isabel looks at the clock for the fourth time in the last half hour, ten more minutes, and she finally closes. She hates working at Christmas, the store becomes a hive of people coming in and out. Many buy for the sake of buying, because it is an obligation marked by consumerism, and then come the returns, which are even worse than last-minute purchases. She takes the microphone and announces over the loudspeaker to all the customers that they are about to close. Of the four people left in the store, three leave to Isabel's relief, and the other, a man with a head strangely disproportionate to the rest of his body, approaches the cash register to pay.

"Have a happy holiday season" said the gentleman kindly.

"You too" Isabel smiles, and it seems that this year she will be able to close on time and get home in time to take a shower, dress for the occasion, and go to the rural house that she and her group of friends in their forties have rented to celebrate Christmas Eve away from the city.

Hopefully she'll hook up with a friend of a friend and get laid tonight. Tomorrow, she will have a headache and will barely remember how a woman ended up by her side. She doesn't care much, she will have indulged herself and then will go back home and continue with her quiet and monotonous life, where no woman will embitter her existence as the last of her lovers did, or try to invade her intimacy prematurely as the previous one did, or want to introduce her to her parents on the second date as the one before the previous did.

When the man walks out the door, Isabel decides that the best thing to do, even though there are still five minutes left, is to lower the shutter to avoid surprises. She's sure her boss won't find out, and if he does, he'll understand that on a special night like this she doesn't feel like going out late like she did many days ago. She is circling the counter to carry out her plan when she sees a woman about her age come in.

"Fuck" she mumbles.

She can't believe her luck, every damn year it's the same.

"Good afternoon" greet the woman hurriedly as she walks past toward the back of the store.

Isabel is in such a bad mood that her reply is barely audible. Marina thinks she's being rude, but she doesn't care because she doesn't intend to spend much time there. She pauses looking in all directions until she visually locates the area where the ties are displayed. She walks over and realizes with annoyance that there are too many to choose from, as indecisive as she is.

Isabel decides that she does not intend to allow any more last minute intrusions, so while she prays for the woman to hurry up, she goes to the entrance, inserts her key in the lock that activates the automatic shutter lock and the shutter begins to lower.

"Hey, I'm still here!" Marina shouts in fear from the back, the last thing she needs is to be locked in the store.

"I know" said Isabel, satisfied for making her uncomfortable, "I'll open the door when you leave, it's closing time, you know?"

"Two minutes left" says Marina, looking at her watch "I'll be done in a minute."

She sighs heavily, she feels the gaze of the impatient sales clerk on the back of her neck and that doesn't help her. She picks up several ties and puts them on some shirts that are hanging in order to compare, she knows that her brother likes light colors for shirts, and she wants to choose one that matches well and that is neither bland nor too serious.

Isabel tries to take it easy and takes the opportunity to gather her things while she waits for the girl to make up her mind. She curses her bad luck, she is always the one who has to take all the trouble. Her partner Antonia left an hour ago because she has three children and it's her turn to cook and prepare everything. Every year it's the same, as she is the single one with no commitments, it's her turn to do the work. She looks at her watch again and despair takes hold of her, it is already two minutes past eight o'clock. Isabel considers herself a patient woman, but not on days like today.

"Do you need my help with anything?" she asks, appearing next to Marina, who is holding three ties in her hands that look practically the same to her.

Isabel assumes that the tie is for the girl's husband and for a moment she thinks how lucky the man is. The woman in front of her has features that Isabel finds very pleasing. She is neither beautiful nor ugly, she is someone from the crowd, but with the particularity of possessing something invisible that is very attractive. She dresses elegantly, but at the same time in a simple or casual way, she does not know how to define her style, but she likes it.

"I just want to choose a tie" Marina replied curtly.

She can't stand going into the stores and being chased by the sales clerks trying to offer her advice. It's annoying, but she understands that the girl behind her back is there, she's wasting a few minutes because of her, and she doesn't think she should be amused.

"Do you have something concrete in mind?" insists Isabel, who does not plan to move from there until the woman leaves.

"No, I'm just looking for one that matches light colors."

Isabel looks at her perplexed at the answer. She knows that black is a godsend for that, so she picks up a black tie and shows it to her, showing her as much kindness as she can.

"You can't go wrong with this one."

"I don't like black, it's too bland, besides, I've never seen my brother with a tie of that color."

So, it is for her brother and not for her husband, Isabel does not know why this clarification has pleased her and that makes her desire to strangle the woman with the black tie diminish a little.

"Maybe a burgundy?" Now Isabel has picked up another tie, one that she will no doubt have to put away in two days when she returns to work, because she certainly doesn't plan to do so now.

"I don't know" Marina hesitates, overwhelmed.

Her eyes wander between the ties she is holding and the one Isabel has, which she also liked.

"Why don't you also give him this shirt? It makes a great combination with the tie, so he won't make a mistake" said Isabel, on the verge of despair.

"I just want to buy a tie" says Marina rudely, her brother has not done so much to spend that money on him.

"Okay, well, I'm sorry, but you'll have to make up your mind now. It's closing time and I'm in a bit of a hurry."

Isabel stands next to Marina and makes a gesture with her hand pointing to the door in a totally shameless way. Marina contains her anger and feels like telling her that she doesn't want one anymore, but if she doesn't come out of there with a tie, her brother will be left without a gift and that will be very embarrassing for her.

"Give me just a second, please" she asks stifled "I'll decide with *Eeny, meeny, miny!*"

"Are you serious?" Isabel asks, trying to figure out if it's a joke.

"I can't think of any other way, you're annoying me and I need to get out of here with a damn tie" spat Marina, whose nerves were getting the better of her."

She has an appointment with her brother at her family's home at ten o'clock and still has to drive almost an hour. If the sales clerk would leave her alone she is sure she would have made up her mind by now, but she keeps looking at her with those eyes that Marina can't guess the exact color, sometimes they seem amber and sometimes brown. They hypnotize her and that distracts her.

"*Eeny, meeny, miny*" She sings to Isabel's astonished gaze, to whom the idea that it might be a hidden camera didn't seem so far-fetched" bam, bam, bam, out!

Marina points her finger at one of the ties for the last time and neither of them has time to see which one it is because the lights in the room suddenly go out.

Chapter 2

"What have you done?" asks Marina, frightened.

"What do you mean, what have I done?" Isabel is indignant, trying to locate her in the darkness, "I haven't done anything.

"What happened?"

"I think it's obvious that the power has gone out" says Isabel, shitting on her bad luck.

The emergency lights on the premises have been turned on, but there are only three, one at each end and one in the center of the fitting rooms. The two of them walk towards the exit door and look through the slits in the shutters to the outside. The darkness is absolute, the shop windows in front of them are turned off and so are the street lamps. It begins to snow.

Isabel takes out her cell phone and turns on the flashlight, Marina imitates her and the two unintentionally blind each other.

"Put that away, for fuck's sake" complains Isabel, who is desperate.

"I'm shining the light on you so you can raise the blind, I need to get out of here right now" says Marina in anguish.

"Do you want to go out now?" Isabel asks, losing her temper, "If we're locked in here it's your fault, if you had decided to get the tie before eight o'clock, we'd both be out by now. Or better yet, you should have stayed out of my store."

"What do you mean, locked up?" interrupts Marina, whose breathing is accelerating, "raise the shutter right now."

"I can't, it's electric, in case you haven't noticed."

Marina looks in all directions in search of another option. It is not that she is afraid or claustrophobic, it is simply that the idea of the privacy of freedom overwhelms her so much, it is enough for her to know that she cannot go out to want to do it with all her strength.

"What about the emergency exit?" she asks, walking down the center aisle toward the back.

"There is no emergency exit" replies Isabel, who, despite how much the situation pisses her off, is enjoying Marina's anguish. According to her, she deserves to suffer for having been so slow.

"All the locals have one" says Marina, who keeps looking, assuming that Isabel has lied to her.

"The new premises, yes, this building is more than a hundred years old in case you haven't noticed, but what are you going to see, if all you can think about is the damn tie that your brother will never wear. How many have you already given him? I'm sure every year the same thing" Isabel can't hold her tongue, all the rage she has been able to contain so far is rushing out of her lips "surely you're a bore who gives the same gifts every year."

Marina turns around and looks at her in the dark. She wants to answer him, but she can't because then she would have to explain that the last two years she spent Christmas Eve alone, that this was the first year she was going out and, now she is locked up with her.

"I'm going to call the fire department to get us out of here" says Marina, feeling proud of her idea.

"The firemen? Of course, I'm sure the poor guys have nothing better to do than come here to get you out. There won't be people locked in elevators or traffic accidents caused by traffic lights going out" Isabel snorts, shaking her head.

Marina is being overcome by the darkness and feeling of confinement, she feels short of breath and anguish is taking over her body. She needs to get out as soon as possible.

"This can't be happening" she laments, walking toward the fitting rooms.

When she arrives, she sits down on the floor, leaning her back against the wall just below the emergency light. It doesn't shine brightly, but it is bright enough to see Isabel's silhouette standing in front of her.

"Are you all right?" The sales clerk asks her, and now the only thing missing is a panic attack. Then she will do everything she can to locate the hidden camera.

"I would be better off out of here."

"And so do I, no shit. I have very interesting plans and none of them included being locked in the store because of an indecisive customer."

"Can you stop attacking me? It's already clear to me how much I've annoyed you" asks Marina, who has just stretched out her legs to see if the cold of the floor can calm her down a little.

"I'm going to call the electric company to ask if this is going to last long" says Isabel.

Marina lets out a derisive snort that Isabel doesn't find funny.

"Do you want to say something to me?"

"Nothing, I wish you luck with your call. If you're waiting for them to take it, you can sit here with me" she says, patting her side.

"What do you mean?" Isabel despairs.

"The whole city seems to be in darkness, I'm sure everyone is calling to find out what the hell has happened. The lines will be saturated and I'm sure they'll keep you on hold, but you can try, I think it's better to listen to those little tunes than to your complaints" Marina lets go, feeling very comfortable.

Isabel snorts resignedly and puts the phone in her pocket. Then she approaches Marina and sits down next to her. When the lights go out, the heating has also been turned off and, the cold starts to set in. The two of them snuggle as close together as they can and take comfort in each other's warmth.

"Look on the bright side, if it gets too cold we have enough clothes to make mattresses on the floor and cover ourselves" says Isabel, trying to lighten the mood.

She has noticed that Marina is getting more and more nervous, she has her hands in her lap and keeps pinching her fingers hard while her feet move as if there is music playing.

"I'm not going to sleep with you" says Marina, not knowing why she said that.

"You'd like it if I slept with you" Isabel swaggers angrily.

Marina turns to her a little puzzled. Suddenly the idea of sleeping with her is not unpleasant for her and she doesn't understand why. The sales clerk seems to her to be a rude person with little patience, but she still has something in her eyes that charms her, even if she can't see it very well now.

The two stare at each other. Isabel's heart beats so furiously that she fears her companion might hear it. The air becomes thick between them and they both think at the same time that, if they have to spend many hours there, it might be better for them to get along with each other.

"What is your name?" Marina doesn't know why she asked that question, it seems like a stupid question at a time like this.

Isabel doesn't answer because she doesn't want to, she remains absorbed in her thoughts imagining what it would be like to kiss this woman.

"I don't know why I'm asking, you're rude and impolite, and you've got it all" Marina said offended.

"I'm rude? You're rude, and inconsiderate too, I wouldn't think of entering a store five minutes before closing time. People like you have no empathy, you think that because this is my job I am obliged to serve you whenever you feel like it."

Again her tongue has shot out and Marina looks at her dumbfounded. She certainly didn't expect a reaction like that and finds it somewhat unconscionable. She's sure the girl has to put up with all kinds of people on a daily basis, but she's not to blame.

Marina feels overwhelmed again, the small conversation with her roommate was distracting her, but it's clear that it's difficult for the two of them to be cordial for more than a minute. So she gets up and goes back to the damn shutter, she's sure there must be some way to open it manually.

"What are you doing?" asks Isabel when she sees her trying to manipulate a box in which she assumes is the electrical box of the shutter.

"What you should do, try to get us out of here."

Marina looks at the painting and sees only switches that serve no purpose. Isabel looks at her and suddenly has a revelation.

"The bathroom window" she let out euphorically.

Marina turns around and looks at her demandingly.

"It's a little high and narrow, but if we manage, we might be able to get out that way. It overlooks a backyard common to a couple of blocks, hopefully, a neighbor will hear us and let us out through their house.

"And why didn't you say so before?"

"Because I couldn't think straight."

Marina looks at her watch, if they get out of there now she still has time to get to dinner with her brother before ten o'clock. Isabel does the same, and if she rules out stopping by her house to take a shower, she'll also get there before those vultures wipe out all the dinner.

Again with their cell phone flashlights on, the two walk to the bathroom, where there is also an emergency light over the door that is totally insufficient. The window Isabel was referring to is the size of a thirty"two inch television set placed vertically in Marina's eyes. In addition, it is at a high height that they cannot access without climbing on something.

"Wait, I'll get the ladder" says Isabel.

She disappears from the bathroom while Marina keeps looking at the window and thinking how small it is. Isabel returns with a small ladder of only three steps.

"Don't you have anything taller?"

"It is what it is" she replies, sighing with impatience.

They place the ladder just below the window. Marina climbs the three steps and checks that the base of the window is at the height of her breasts. She opens it and looks out with the flashlight of her cell phone. There is indeed a courtyard outside, but the jump from the window to the ground is almost two meters, not to mention that they would have to jump headfirst.

"I don't see it clearly" she mumbles in disappointment.

Isabel asks her to step aside while nodding her head, thinking that she is not only indecisive but also a bit of a coward, but when she looks out she can see with her own eyes that the client is right. She looks from one side to the other in desperation, if she doesn't get out of there as soon as possible, she can't be sure that she won't end up fulfilling her desire to strangle the woman with the black tie. She looks up and sees a ledge above the window, maybe if she manages to sit on the base and hold on to the ledge with her hands, she can manage to position herself in a way that allows her to hang down with some security.

"There is a way out, but you'd better do it yourself."

"Me? Why don't you do it?" Marina complains.

"Because I have the fattest ass and this is very narrow, it's easier for you to get out and then help me from the other side."

Marina's eyes fly to Isabel's buttocks hopelessly, maybe she has some extra pounds, but in her opinion it is very well distributed and makes her figure very slender and attractive.

She decides not to protest because all that is time wasted and she doesn't have much left.

Marina climbs the three steps and follows Isabel's instructions. She supports herself with her hands to give herself a boost and with the help of the sales clerk who puts her hands intertwined as a step so that she can support one foot, she manages to sit at the base of the window with her legs dangling towards the inside of the bathroom.

"Now you have to hold on to the ledge, squat at the base and drop down to the other side.

"What ledge, if I can't see?" Marina protests in complete tension "could you at least illuminate me with the flashlight"

"Oh, yes, sorry" says Isabel, who tries to hold in her laughter.

The sales clerk also climbs the three steps of the small staircase and suddenly finds herself between Marina's knees. The situation makes her nervous, if someone were to see them right now, besides thinking they have stolen something and pretending to flee in a rather strange way through the window, they might also think they are entertaining themselves in other ways.

"I'm going to have to touch you to get your arm out of the window" says Isabel.

"I don't bite" Marina is offended again.

Isabel nods in amusement at how surreal the whole situation seems to her since that woman has walked through the door of the store. She places a hand behind Marina's knee to support herself and Marina gives a jump because she didn't expect it. The movement throws Isabel off balance and, while she lets out at least twelve curses through her mouth, she grabs Marina's waist with both hands and sinks her face between her legs trying to keep her balance so that the ladder doesn't tip over under her feet.

"What are you doing, you pervert?" Marina gets scared and stiffens up.

It should be noted that Marina has part of her body outside the window and can no longer see inside the bathroom.

"Pervert? You almost got me killed" says the sales clerk when she regains control.

Her heart beats a thousand per hour, she doesn't know if it's because of the fright or because of the proximity to the other woman, maybe a mixture of both. When Isabel is about to sit up again, the cell phone, which she had miraculously managed to hold between two fingers, slips out of her hand and falls to the floor.

"Shit!" she shouts outraged without letting go of Marina's waist.

"What is it now?" despairs Marina, who is freezing and can barely feel her fingers.

"I dropped my cell phone, wait."

Marina snorts as Isabel tries not to kill herself as she descends the steps in the dark. She grabs Marina's knees again and gropes her way to the next step with her foot, since the flashlight on her cell phone has gone out with the blow, and the emergency light and a flashlight with dead batteries seem the same to her.

"If you don't hurry up, I'm going to turn into a Marina polo shirt."

"Don't push me, okay? You can't see anything in here."

"And out here, yes?" Now Marina thinks about the bugs that might lurk above her head and feels a shiver that makes her shake again, luckily, Isabel has just set foot on the ground and already feels safe.

Just as the sales clerk glances at the floor in search of her cell phone, the light comes back on, illuminating everything.

"Hallelujah!" shouts Isabel, overjoyed.

"Stop with the hallelujahs and help me get down from here."

Chapter 3

It took Marina relatively little time to climb up to the window, but coming down, that's another story. It's like when you climb a tree, and you feel like a monkey because of your amazing agility, but when it's time to climb down you feel like an asshole because you don't understand how you could have climbed up there without having a plan to get down. Leaning back a bit, you look around the inside of the bathroom and can't think of any way to get down without falling and leaving your back. You stretch as far as you can, trying to reach the first rung of the ladder with one foot, but it's impossible.

"Okay, wait, I'll put your hands back on and support your foot" says Isabel.

Marina feels the support of Isabel's hands, but in this position she cannot see what she is doing or what is coming next, and that generates a distrust that paralyzes her with fear and makes her not dare to support herself at all.

"Come on, woman, with the luck we have, the power is still on again" Isabel snorts impatiently.

"Don't push me" Marina complains, "I'd like to see you up here having to go down blind"

"Okay, we'll move on to plan B."

"Plan B?" asks Marina.

"Yes."

"And what is it?

Suddenly, Marina notices Isabel's hands on the back of her thighs and tenses like a bowstring.

"Let yourself fall little by little, I promise I won't let go."

"How can I let go? Are you crazy? You can't handle me" Marina panics when she sees Marina pulling on her.

"It's not about me holding you in my arms either, just holding you while you let go so that you go down slowly and don't get a slap on the floor. Come on, fuck it, it's Christmas, a little adventurous spirit"

"At Christmas you have Christmas spirit, not adventurousness" Marina corrects her.

"Whatever you say, either you drop or I swear I'll leave you here and get out" Isabel threatens without taking her hands off her thighs.

Marina closes her eyes tightly and lets herself fall little by little, she doesn't trust the woman below her, but under the circumstances it's better to accept her help and pray that everything goes well, than to let herself fall and skin her back and ass with the base of the window.

Isabel squeezes Marina's thighs tightly to try to keep her as close to her as possible and thus exercise better control, but as she slides, her hands move up the customer's legs until, hopelessly, she ends up grabbing her buttocks. Marina tenses her ass cheeks and her whole body as soon as she feels the sales clerk's hands on her buttocks. Isabel senses how hard that part of Marina's body has become with her touch and tries not to think about it more than necessary, because she likes the sensation and in other circumstances and if she were someone more accessible and less disconcerting than this woman, she would love to continue exploring. At last, Marina lets herself fall at last and Isabel's arms hold her close to her body as she puts her feet on the floor. The closeness catches them both so off guard that neither is able to react sensibly. Marina feels the sales clerk's hands hovering tightly around her waist and she can't take her eyes off her lips, which remain half open and glossy. Isabel's heart is pounding, and her blood has rushed to the same place, she feels an enormous temptation to kiss this woman whose name she doesn't even know and who seems to have been sent to ruin her Christmas Eve.

"I must go" says Marina, finally breaking the silence.

Isabel lets go as if she had received an electric shock and separates a little embarrassed at the thought that perhaps her client has interpreted it as an attempt to take advantage.

"Yes, me too."

The two go out into the store, Isabel in front and Marina behind, who bends down to pick up her purse from the floor and hangs it over her shoulder with an elegance that fascinates Isabel in a way that baffles her.

"Well, I'm sorry for the inconvenience I've caused you" Marina apologized."

"Go now" says Isabel, making a hand gesture with her hand as if shooing away a fly.

After that, she goes to the shutter and inserts the key to make it go up, so as not to run the risk of another blackout and get locked inside again. Marina reaffirms that the sales clerk is very rude, but she doesn't intend to waste time reminding her. She buttons her coat while Isabel goes to the other side of the counter to get her purse and heads for the exit to get the hell out of there.

"Wait" asks Isabel, raising her voice.

Marina, who already has one foot on the street and has heard the snow crunching under her soles, turns around and looks at her in bewilderment, just hoping she doesn't intend to give her two kisses after how rude she has been to her.

"You forgot this" says Isabel, running to her.

Marina doesn't see what she's holding in her hand until it's in front of her. It's the tie that won the *Eeny, meeny, miny.*

"I don't have time to pay for it now, if I don't leave now, I won't make it" Marina answers in a hurry.

"I don't have time to spend charging you for it either, take it and come back another day to pay for it, but do it, because if you don't, they'll deduct it from my salary and for thirty euros I swear I'll look for you even under the stones" Isabel threatens.

Although she is a strange woman whose behavior she cannot understand, Marina thanks the sales clerk with a sincere smile that she has not been able to control and accepts the tie.

"Thank you, some wrapping paper would be too much to ask for, wouldn't it?" jokes Marina, pushing her luck.

"I'm sure you can think of something, now get out of here before you jinx me some more" Isabel says, opening the light box to turn everything off before closing it.

Marina waves goodbye and hurries across the street after assuring her that she will be back to pay for the tie. Isabel watches her run carefully in the snow, which fortunately has not set, and surprises herself with the hope that Marina will keep her word and come back for the store.

Chapter 4

Marina walks to the parking lot as fast as she can considering that the sidewalk is starting to slip. Snowflakes fall on her shoulders and crumble on her coat. She regrets forgetting to take the umbrella, but, after all, the subway parking is not that far away either, and seeing the street adorned with Christmas lights and music blaring from the speakers while a few clueless people like her walk in a hurry, gives her a feeling of nostalgia that makes her feel good. The reality is, she has always loved the Christmas season and for a while she cursed Elisa for leaving her at a time like this. Not only because of the pain it caused her, but also because it clouded a time of the year that she enjoyed very much.

Sh slips and curses between her teeth, luckily she manages to keep her balance and finally arrives at the parking lot. She walks slowly down the wide steps of the ramp and as she pulls out her card to go pay, decides that she plans to enjoy this Christmas to the fullest, starting with dinner with her brother and nephews' pigs.

When she finally gets to the car, she takes off her coat and spreads it out on the back seat to dry out the moisture from the flakes that have melted on it. She turns the heater on full blast to regain the warmth she lost while she was in the store and wastes a couple of minutes calling her brother and telling him that she might be a little late. She briefly explains the episode in the store and her brother finds it so surreal that he finally admits that she couldn't possibly have made it up.

"Asshole" mumbles smiling.

Marina starts the engine and pulls out of her parking space, yields to a car and heads for the exit. There are very few cars left inside. It is almost nine o'clock and the normal, foresighted people are already at home with their families getting ready for dinner, only she, with her haste, is the one who will be late.

When she gets near the exit she gets nervous, the barrier is up because apparently there is a breakdown and the parking attendant is on one side checking that they have paid. Marina is reminded of the queue at *Mc Auto*, where those guys go from car to car taking orders. Here it's the same, a small queue has formed in which she was the last one until another car pulls up behind her.

The cars are leaving little by little and as she gets closer she realizes that the ramp is much steeper than she expected, in addition, in this short time, the snow has begun to fall with more intensity and is curdling. She watches with anxiety as one of the cars stops in the middle of the climb because it has skidded and has to give a strong acceleration to get out successfully. Marina tenses up, she doesn't like extreme conditions, let alone having to make maneuvers like that with the car. The vehicle in front of her is next, and after the parking attendant indicates something to the driver, the driver gets out at a higher speed than normal and drives up the ramp at once. Now the attendant approaches her and Marina rolls down the window.

"The ramp is starting to slip, climb it at once, don't slow down and you won't have any problems" recommends the man.

Marina is about to get out of the car and ask him to get in, but her pride does not allow her to do so, although she is afraid of the situation, she knows she can do it, so she looks ahead, and decisively accelerates.

Isabel listens to what the parking attendant says and looks him up and down a little offended. She has already figured out on her own what to do if she wants to go up the parking ramp, but she thanks him for his advice with a fake smile and rolls up the window. As soon as the car in front of her accelerates, she accelerates behind it, ignoring whatever the attendant is shouting at her. She does so because never in her worst dreams would she have imagined that the person in front of her would think of braking in the middle of the ramp. Isabel also brakes and both vehicles come to a standstill in the worst possible position. Marina is very nervous, everything was going well until she saw a person cross in front of her car just as she was about to get to the top, obviously, she braked immediately and was lucky that the car didn't skid. She suddenly warmed up. If she was nervous before, now she is about to spit her heart out of her mouth. She has been left in a really unfavorable position, standing in the middle of a steep ramp while it's snowing, and for dessert she has a car behind her.

Marina feels overwhelmed and wants to get out of there as soon as possible. She takes a couple of breaths to try to calm her heart rate and without thinking about it, because she knows that if she takes too many turns she won't dare, she pulls the handbrake, puts the car in first gear and grips the steering wheel tightly, as if this would give her more control over the car. When she feels ready, she lowers the handbrake and sinks her foot on the accelerator, she does it with so much emphasis that instead of going out little by little as in her imagination, the wheels skid without moving and Marina sees without remedy how her car goes backwards and impacts against the one that was stopped behind her.

Isabel starts honking her horn hysterically as if that would prevent what has just happened. She can't believe her bad luck, with how well she had started the day and how badly she is ending it. Marina, who is so nervous that she doesn't even know what she's doing, takes advantage of the fact that her car is leaning against the one behind her and accelerates out of the parking lot, this time successfully.

"Holy fuck!" Isabel shouts from her car, thinking that she has the nerve to run away. When she tries to accelerate to follow her, the front of her car makes an awful noise and the attendant yells at her not to continue up the ramp, to let her slowly drop down the ramp and park the car.

Isabel obeys fearing the worst and she is not wrong, because when she gets out, her front bumper is broken in the middle and one of the parts is hanging so that it is scraping the ground. Marina manages to merge into the lane and as the street is deserted, she parks the car and gets out to check the damage. Her car has nothing on it and that surprises her, because she heard a loud crunch on impact, so if it wasn't her car, it had to be the other one. That's all she needed, to waste more time filling out an accident report.

She puts on her coat and, careful not to slip, begins to descend the ramp. As soon as she sees the other car she opens her mouth in surprise at the damage.

"Mother, I'm so sorry" says as she approaches.

Isabel turns at that moment because the voice she has heard sounds familiar and she needs to check with her own eyes that the person responsible for making her car look like a chrome car is the same person who, with her indecision in the store, has ensured that the power outage still caught them together.

"Satan sent you to harvest my soul?" she says, still in disbelief.

Marina watches her perplexed without understanding how it is possible for them to meet twice in such a short period of time and on top of that have the bad luck to have a collision with the cars.

"Is it yours?" She knows the question is stupid before she finishes saying it, but she's so surprised that it's the first thing that came to her.

"No, it's from Santa Claus" says Isabel with sparks in her eyes.

Marina doesn't know what to say and just watches Isabel, who circles around the car without quite believing what she sees.

"Are you sure it can't be fixed?" asks Marina to say something.

"Sure, we put a little glue on it and that's it" Isabel spits out.

"Hey, don't be so rude, if you hadn't been glued to my ass this wouldn't have happened" Marina was indignant.

"No, now it's going to be my fault that you don't know how to drive."

"Peace, ladies" says the parking attendant, whose closing time is also approaching, "you can leave the car here and send a tow truck to pick it up tomorrow, we won't charge you anything" proposes to Isabel.

"She may want to charge me" Isabel protested out of her mind, "that little bitch comes down on me and wrecks my car in her crappy parking lot, and for her to want to charge me would be the last straw"

"Madam, please relax."

"Isabel puts her hand to her chest, consumed by anxiety, and Marina approaches her to try to calm her down, even though she is aware that she is not the person the sales clerk wants to see the most"

"Listen, we'll make the report and order a cab to take you wherever you need to go, I'll pay for it" proposes in a conciliatory tone.

Isabel looks at her trying to calm her pulse. She would like to yell at her for what she thinks about the way she is driving, but her civic minded side makes her behave, because she recognizes that the woman has not done it on purpose, and since they have the brown on top of them, the cab option is the most reasonable one.

"All right, I'll call the cab. Do you have accident reports?"

"Yes, of course" replies Marina, calmer when she sees that the sales clerk has stopped shouting.

"Wait" says the manager, "would you mind filling it out and waiting outside? I don't want to seem inconsiderate, but I must close up now or my wife will throw me out of the house if I'm late for dinner."

The two turn round to him to yell at him what they haven't yelled at each other, but the man looks so distraught, they both give in and, after Isabel grabs her purse and a bag from her car, the two leave the parking lot and get into Marina's car to fill out the paperwork and call the cab.

Marina opens the glove compartment and takes out the folder where she keeps the documentation. Isabel watches her run her fingers through the papers while she waits for someone on the other end of the line to answer, but she keeps on talking. Marina can't find what she's looking for and takes the papers out of the folder so she can examine them better. Finally, someone decides to answer, but Isabel is told that all the cabs on duty that night are on a service and that they won't be able to pick her up for another forty-five minutes.

"Forty five minutes?" Isabel repeats incredulously.

She looks at her watch, it's after a quarter past nine, by the time she gets there, her bitchy friends will not only have devastated the food, but they'll already be a little impaired by the alcohol and she'll have a hard time adjusting to the party. She hangs up the phone and throws her head back in her seat admitting defeat while Marina continues to search through her papers in desperation, until she remembers that she has no report because she gave the one she had to a girl who had a blow in front of her and hasn't replaced it.

"I don't have any left" she announces, fearful of her companion's reaction.

Isabel drops her head to her side as if she has died and has a fit of hysterical laughter. Her customer's jinx has no parts and her car is now locked in the parking lot until tomorrow. Marina doesn't know whether to laugh or cry, the sales clerk's laughter makes her nervous because she fears that at any moment she will suddenly shut up and start yelling at her, but that's not what happens.

"Can you drop me off at my house? I don't live far" asks Isabel after a deep sigh.

Marina can, of course, but she feels bad that she screwed up his plans even though she still thinks that what happened on that ramp wasn't just her fault.

"Where were you going? Maybe I'm on my way."

When the sales clerk explains where she intended to go, Marina is stuck in her seat.

"Really? I'm going there too" she explains, still puzzled.

Isabel opens her eyes like headlights, she's not one to believe in fate or anything like that, but she begins to think that, for some reason, that night the stars are aligning to keep them together longer than they should.

"But it's a village in the middle of nowhere, there are only rural houses there" Isabel answered, puzzled.

"I know, my grandparents had a farmhouse there that my mother inherited and almost every year the whole family gets together there, except this year my parents have decided to go on a cruise with my aunt and uncle and only my brother and I will be there.

Marina thinks she has just explained too much, but the woman's presence makes her nervous, and when that happens, she is just as likely to remain absolutely silent as to let out her tongue.

"My name is Isabel" the sales clerk introduced herself, extending her hand with some trepidation.

Marina tells her name and then squeezes her. They both let go quickly because they feel a certain discomfort that they don't know where it comes from, and as if they are in rapport, they both look at their watches. If they leave now and nothing else happens to them, they can arrive at a reasonable time.

Chapter 5

Marina uses the GPS navigator because she only goes to town once in a while, so she never quite remembers the way. They leave the town with relative ease and join the main road. The machines have been pouring salt and the passage of vehicles has left the lane clear, but it is still snowing and Marina is very apprehensive.

Isabel takes the opportunity to call her friends and tell them that she won't be too late, that she is starving. Marina hears the laughter in the background through the phone and feels a slight pang of envy, it is clear that Isabel is going to have a much better time than her that night. They are sure to have a good time while she is in the family home listening to the three pigs singing Christmas carols.

"How will you get back tomorrow?" Marina asks to break the silence when Isabel hangs up.

"With one of my friends, I guess" she answers without further ado.

Marina, despite being a quiet and calm woman, does not like silences, especially if she has to walk for more than half an hour with a person she hardly knows and with whom she has already lived a couple of unpleasant experiences. Hopefully, her nephews will fall asleep by one o'clock at the latest and she will be able to enjoy a quiet and boring chat with her brother and sister-in-law until she gets sleepy.

After twenty minutes of absolute silence where only the music of the radio that Isabel has asked permission to turn on has been playing, they take the detour to the village. The road becomes narrow, dark and full of curves, and to top it off, it is a shady area due to the height of the mountains that rise next to it, so that several areas remain frozen most of the winter. Marina knows this fact, but Isabel does not and starts to move her leg nervously when Marina slows down considerably. She holds back and says nothing, but after five minutes and seeing that things seem to be getting worse, she begins to despair and lets out a snort that angers Marina.

"Is something wrong?" she asks without looking at her.

"Nothing, it's just that if you keep slowing down I think we'll get there sooner on foot" says Isabel, trying not to sound too rude.

"The road is icy, so I'll go as slowly as I can. If you don't like it, you get out and walk, if you want I'll lower the window and you can tell me how your feet get cold and all that.

Marina has been as rude as she could. She is beginning to be very fed up with Isabel, she is a woman who really disconcerts her, and the worst of all is that, although she can't stand her, she doesn't dislike having her by her side either. It is a contradictory feeling that she cannot understand and that frustrates her, and to make matters worse, it begins to snow more heavily.

"How long has it been since you've been out? I mean to let loose" asks Isabel, leaving Marina confused, who doesn't understand what the question is about.

"Why do you want to know?"

"Because I think it would be good for you to relax a little, you're biting at the drop of a hat.

Isabel is very proud of how fine she has been, because in reality, what she wanted to tell her is that she always seems to have a stick up her ass, but she has controlled herself because she doesn't want to make her more nervous and end Christmas Eve in a ditch with her.

"I don't think my leisure time is any of your business" Marina replied irritably.

"You see? That's because it's been so long that you don't even remember, I'm sure you're just a deadbeat" she accuses her with every intention of provoking her.

Marina, despite her patience, falls right into Isabel's trap and enters into her game.

"I'd rather be a goner than crazy when I'm forty.

"I haven't fulfilled them yet" said Isabel offended.

Marina laughs. She doesn't know why, but Isabel's reaction makes her laugh and as she notices that her laughter bothers her, she laughs even harder. Isabel turns up the music so as not to hear her, but Marina turns it down from the steering wheel controls and finally, Isabel ends up turning off the radio to have the last word and they both end up laughing their heads off.

Amidst laughter and absurd discussions, the last few minutes have flown by and they have arrived in town. Marina follows the directions to the house that Isabel has told her and realizes that the rural house where her strange companion will be staying tonight is only two streets away from hers.

"Well, we're close" she mutters louder than she meant to.

"Is your house around here?" Isabel asks curiously.

"A couple of blocks away."

"Well, thank you very much for the ride, what do you say we exchange numbers and I'll call you tomorrow afternoon to make the report?" Isabel proposes before getting out of the car.

"Of course"

The two take out their respective phones and write down each other's number. When they put them away, it creates one of those awkward moments that they would both like to run away from without having to say anything.

"Well, have a good time with your family" Isabel finally says.

"And you with your friends."

"Surely better than you, I mean, well..." Isabel tries to fix it, realizing that the comment was out of place.

Marina wants to say something that hurts her as much as it has hurt her, but the words choke in her mouth and refuse to come out. Isabel notices her discomfort and doesn't know what to do to fix her stupidity, her mother always tells her that there are times when she should bite her tongue, and this has certainly been one of them.

"I'm sorry" she apologized, "I didn't mean to be so rude."

"Thank you for the tie, now if you'll excuse me, I'm late."

Isabel gets out of the car feeling guilty, closes the door and waves goodbye, but Marina does not return the gesture and simply drives off. As she walks towards the entrance of the house she thinks about how she can fix her screw up and, at the same time, she feels strange not understanding why she has this need to fix things with the woman who almost ruined her Christmas Eve.

Chapter 6

The dinner at Marina's family home with her brother, her sister-in-law and the children went much better than she expected. Now the three older ones have just made a toast that they will all get together again the following year and as Marina imagined, the three little ones are bawling their heads off, but it doesn't bother her, on the contrary, she is enjoying it very much. She has her niece, the youngest of five years old, on her lap, and Marina, at the girl's request, bangs a tambourine while the little one pierces her eardrums and turns red from the effort because she wants to be heard above the voice of her siblings.

When the little girl can't take it anymore, she ends up falling asleep on her aunt while the others continue singing until they get bored and play on the carpet. Her middle niece colors a mandala and her oldest nephew sets up a curvy car-parking track that Marina has given him. When she sees it, the memory of Isabel hits him hard and she wonders what she is doing at that moment. She imagines her laughing non-stop with her friends and to her surprise, even though she is a woman who disturbs her a lot with her unpredictable behavior, she wishes she is having a good time.

Isabel has eaten her dinner to bursting. Now they are having an after-dinner conversation, all of them talking and laughing while drinking cava and eating Christmas sweets. As they haven't seen each other for days, they all explain their anecdotes except Isabel, who only listens or pretends to, because she thinks she could explain what happened to Marina that afternoon and she is sure it would be a story that would make them all laugh. They would make jokes without bad intentions accusing Marina of being a bit of a jinx and for some reason that Isabel cannot understand, she does not want them to laugh at her, not even as a joke.

"Let me refill your glass, you're very dull" says Luisa, her best friend's cousin, whom she has seen on one occasion or another and with whom she had a one-night stand the last time they saw each other.

Luisa is very attentive to her, she does it cautiously and without overwhelming her because she knows that Isabel does not like her space to be invaded or pressured, but Isabel is not in favor of it, even though she came with the intention of going to sleep accompanied, either by Luisa or by any guest of her friends with whom she would have understood.

"Thank you" she replies with a warm smile.

She picks up her glass to take a sip, but Luisa steps forward and proposes a toast, Isabel has not quite understood what she said because they all speak at the same time and it is difficult to follow a conversation. She knocks her glass with Luisa and drinks the liquid almost in one gulp, and then, without really knowing why, she finds herself with her cell phone in her hand and the WhatsApp open with Marina's name. Her heart pounding hard. She doesn't understand what's happening to her, but now that she's a little tipsy from the cava, the only thing she wants to do is see her. She thinks that maybe it's because she feels guilty for the unfortunate comment she made before getting out of the car and that what she needs to do is apologize to her. Be that as it may, when she realizes it, her fingers move nimbly writing sentences that she later erases because they don't convince her.

"Who are you talking to?" asks Aitana, who sits on the other side of her and has been watching her friend fighting with her cell phone for a while.

"With a friend who has a house right here, I was thinking of telling her to come by for a drink" she replies, surprised by her sincerity.

"Of course, the more the better, is she pretty?" Asked a girl whose name she couldn't remember and whom she suddenly didn't like very much.

Isabel ignores her and stands up, determined to call Marina and put an end to her indecision. She will propose, and if she says no, at least she won't feel so bad and she will be able to get rid of that feeling of guilt that has haunted her since they said goodbye. She snorts in obfuscation, she does not understand why she is so affected by what her words may have provoked in that woman, after all, she hardly knows her and it is clear to her that the farther away she has her, the better. In one afternoon, more strange things have happened to her than during the rest of the year.

Marina has placed her hand on her niece's face, covering her ear and at the same time holding it to her chest so that the noise doesn't wake her up. She sees the screen of her cell phone on the table light up and start to ring. Her brother, who is a total gossip, leans forward to see who is calling her and Marina does too. Her heart skips a beat when she sees Isabel's name on the screen, she still doesn't know why she has taken the trouble to record it if the only thing she has left to do with her is the accident report, but she has done it, and now she knows that for some unknown reason, Isabel wants to talk to her.

"You will not take the call?" asks her brother with a sly smile.

Marina warms up and has become nervous, she doesn't know why, but she doesn't want to talk to Isabel in front of them.

"I'll call her now" she announced, getting to her feet carefully so as not to wake her niece.

Her sister-in-law Maribel follows her to the room where the children sleep when they go and between the two of them they put the little one to bed.

"Any friends?" Maribel asks in a whisper as they are leaving the room.

"We are not friends, I met her this afternoon by chance and she happens to be celebrating Christmas Eve next door with some friends.

"What a coincidence, isn't it?"

"Well, yes" Marina cut her off, not wanting to go deeper into the conversation.

When they return to the dining room, Marina picks up her cell phone and goes to the kitchen to return the call.

Isabel has returned to sit next to Luisa with some disappointment after Marina didn't pick up the phone. She thinks of several possibilities for why she didn't pick up the phone, that she is angry with her for what she has said or that she is already sleeping. The first option makes her feel strange, the second one hurts her in an incomprehensible way and the third one makes her laugh alone, but no one notices because they all do it one way or another.

"They're calling you, Isabel" says Luisa, pointing to her cell phone.

Isabel gives a gasp when she sees Marina's name, with the noise she didn't hear it ringing and quickly picks it up so as not to cut the call.

"Hello" she shouts louder than she intended as she gets up and walks away to a quiet area.

"Hello" said Marina, a little curtly, "I saw your call."

Isabel really likes the way Marina's voice sounds on the phone, and that's worrying.

"Yes. I didn't wake you up, did I?"

Isabel immediately regrets her question and feels stupid. How could she be such an imbecile as to put her foot in her mouth again? Although she feels terrible about it, this time Marina didn't mind, because she didn't notice that mocking tone with which Isabel spoke to her earlier.

"No, although I don't think it will take long" admits after hiding a yawn.

"Come and have a drink here" Isabel proposes at once.

Marina is so surprised by the offer that she can't give a quick answer and keeps silent while she thinks about whether she is really inviting her or just trying to tease her. Isabel seems to be one of those explosive women that you never know where they are going to come from, at least that is the impression she has given her since they met.

"Can you hear me well?" asks Isabel cautiously.

"Yes, I heard you."

"So, would you like to come?" insists the sales clerk.

"I don't know, I don't know anyone there" says Marina, who is suffocating with doubts about whether Isabel is inviting her out of pure commitment.

"You know me, and the others are nice girls, at least the ones I know"

"I thank you for the invitation, Isabel, but I don't want to bother you and I don't want you to feel obliged to put up with me"

"I called you because I wanted to, not because I had to" Isabel answers a little annoyed, "come on, come, have a drink and if you don't feel comfortable, leave. What have you got to lose?"

"All right" agrees Marina nervously.

"Perfect, hurry up, I'll wait for you at the door, with all the fuss they're making I won't hear the doorbell"

When Marina hangs up, her pulse is racing and she can't think of what to do next. Her brother and sister-in-law are already asking her nieces and nephews to get ready for bed, so she tells them that she has a date with the mysterious friend on the phone, grabs her coat and without thinking much more, walks out the door.

Chapter 7

For a change, Marina has not thought to take the umbrella, luckily for her, the intensity of the snowfall has reduced and she does not think she will get very wet. When she arrives at the house where she left Isabel a few hours ago, she sees her at the front door with her arms wrapped around her body to keep out the cold, she doesn't have an umbrella either and that makes Marina feel a little less awkward.

"Hello" Isabel says as soon as she sees her.

Marina stops in front of her, not knowing what to do. Once again an awkward situation arises between the two of them and Isabel thinks that maybe it was not a good idea to invite her. Marina is very restrained and she is too direct, two very different ways of being and perhaps the reason why they are arguing at the drop of a hat.

"It's cold" says Marina by way of greeting.

Isabel decides that she does not want these tense situations between them and that she is going to personally take care of them and cut them off before they become too uncomfortable, so she approaches Marina and gives her two kisses of those that are given with desire, the surprise is that Marina gives them back to her.

"Let's go inside, I'll introduce you to my friends and we'll have a drink, inside you'll warm up right away, they've overheated" says Isabel as they cross the courtyard.

As they enter the foyer Marina agrees that the heating is too high, she immediately feels that her coat is too much and her cheeks burn from the temperature contrast. She leaves it hanging on a coat rack that Isabel indicates to her and together they go to the dining room, where at least ten women are dancing and fooling around in front of the television, which is broadcasting one of those Christmas programs in which singers of all kinds are constantly appearing.

Isabel lowers the heating thermostat wheel a couple of degrees and then announces the presence of her new friend. They all turn towards them, making Marina feel a little self-conscious, but she gets over it quickly, because they are all around her age and immediately make her feel comfortable. Isabel pours her a glass of cava and the two of them toast together.

"Thank you for inviting me" Marina says after taking another sip.

"You are welcome."

The music continues to play and the two women move discreetly following the rhythm, until Isabel takes the initiative and pulls Marina towards the center of the dining room, where they are all dancing like crazy. They have turned down the TV and put on their own music to liven up the party. Marina has another drink, and this, added to the previous one and the one she had at home with her family, begins to have an effect on her. She feels more uninhibited and begins to enjoy herself like she hasn't done in a long time. Isabel has stepped aside because she needs to catch her breath. She pours herself a glass of soda to avoid getting drunk and just watches Marina. Now she no longer seems to him a bland and boring woman, and she has just discovered that she has a very nice smile that, added to that intense gleam in her eyes, is hypnotizing Isabel as if she were a snake charmer.

"Do you have something with her?" Luisa's question, suddenly appearing at her side, puts her completely off her game.

"No, no, we're just friends" she answers, embarrassed to get out of the way.

She doesn't know why that question has made her so nervous, but she gets much worse with Luisa's answer.

"Then you won't mind if I go in, will you?" I think she understands.

Isabel nods her head without articulating a word and watches in horror as Luisa goes straight to Marina and grabs her around the waist to dance. She doesn't know what bothers her more, that Luisa has passed her by in such a blatant way or that she has decided to walk in on Marina. She is not sure whether Marina understands or not, she is such a woman of her own that Isabel finds it hard to pick up on the signals.

Luisa doesn't give Marina much respite, so under the excuse that she needs a drink, the snake charmer stops and grabs her cup from the table.

"Do you want me to put another one on you?" Luisa offers, and although she tries not to be overwhelming, Marina is starting to get annoyed. She has already insinuated herself to her a couple of times and she has pretended to be a Swede, she is one of those who believes that a few words are enough, but it seems that Luisa does not give up and without knowing why, she looks for Isabel with her eyes and makes a gesture to ask for her help.

Isabel bites her cheeks to keep from jumping with excitement. She got Marina's message the first time and feels a relief that she doesn't understand when she sees that she doesn't feel the slightest interest in Luisa.

She then takes Marina by the arm and leads her to the corner where she has remained until now

"Thank you" says Marina, closing her eyes for a second to enjoy the peace of mind that comes with not being in the middle of all.

She's having a great time, but she can't stand being around people for too long. She needs to take short breaks to clear her head before continuing to dance.

"I'm sorry she bothered you, Luisa can be a little intense at times, but she's a good aunt" Isabel defends her.

"I like Luisa, Isabel" she says, "I'm just not interested in having anything with her and I don't want her to think that something is going to happen between us"

"The naturalness with which Marina has spoken about the possibility of flirting with a woman, makes her see that Luisa was right and it is very possible that Marina also understands.

"You have some very nice friends."

Isabel nods and glances at the center of the dining room, where little by little they have been dispersing and instead of dancing, they talk to each other.

"What do you do for a living?" Isabel asks.

Marina looks at her surprised by the interest and Isabel fears that it may have come across as an impertinent or personal question, she is so secretive that she has to grope blindly to see where her limits are.

"It's to be on equal terms" adds Isabel when she sees that Marina is slow to answer, "it's obvious that you know where I work, but I don't know anything about you"

"Do you want to know things about me?"

Isabel's cheeks suddenly burn and Marina smiles with satisfaction at the result of the pearl that she has suddenly dropped on her with full intention.

"I'm trying to be nice" said Isabel, realizing that if they continue down this path they will soon be arguing.

Marina, who is also aware of this clash of character between them, does not want to take the situation to the limit because she has realized that as much as it surprises her and is hard to understand, she likes being with Isabel.

"I'm a secretary in a humble law firm. I am in charge of the telephone, arranging visits and invoices, among other things" she explains to calm the tension that always grows between them.

Isabel has no trouble imagining Marina sitting at the reception desk of that office, showing visitors in or taking calls. She is a perfect woman for that, elegant, discreet and polite.

"Let's play!" shouts one of the women, making the two women look in her direction.

The girl in question, whose name is Cristina, appears with a cardboard box on which she has drawn the face of what she pretends to be a reindeer and on top of which she has put two wooden branches to simulate the antlers.

"What game is that?" asks Marina, intrigued and at the same time amused by how lame the invention is.

"I have no idea, I don't even know when she has spent the time to make such a work of art" Isabel answers.

They both laugh and approach the others to listen to Cristina's explanation of the rules of the game while the music continues to play in the background. She has the area cleared and has placed the box on a chair next to the television. From a bag she pulls out several plastic rings and Isabel is surprised that they are real and not made by her out of aluminum foil or clay.

"Okay, it's very easy, we stand behind this line" explains Cristina, pointing to one of the joints in the floor, "and from here, we have to throw the hoops and manage to get them into the reindeer's antlers"

They all consider the game quite childish, but they don't say anything because Cristina seems very excited and, besides, she has taken the time to make such a work of art, which none of the others have done.

"And what's in it for us? Seems a bit dull" says Luisa cautiously.

"It's not so dull if every time you don't get it right you have to take off an article of clothing" Cristina said, surprising those present. She has just turned a simple, childish game into something that can be extremely fun for a group of adult women who are a little impaired by drinking.

"We establish an order and each one throws, if done right, she remains dressed, if fails, she takes off a garment. When you get to the underwear, you are eliminated completely, we are not going to turn this into a porn movie. Obviously, the winner is the one who lasts the longest with her clothes on"

Marina's heart beats fast, but Isabel is eager to start playing.

"Are you up for it?"

"I don't know" says Marina, cut off, "maybe I should..."

"Of course she'll be happy" Cristina intervenes, "we all have the same thing here, don't we?" she asks, grabbing her breasts"come on, it'll be fun"

A girl named Nerea pours some shot glasses for everyone. Isabel and Marina drink it in one gulp and smile at each other in an innocent and almost adolescent way that makes them both nervous. Cristina establishes a queue order, turns up the music a little to liven up the atmosphere and the first of them makes some provocative hip movements until she throws the ring. As expected, she misses.

Chapter 8

They all laugh and cheer, urging her to take off the garment. The girl takes off her turtleneck sweater and throws it on the sofa. The next in line throws and when she misses, she complains that she felt pressured by the others and that's why she missed. Marina watches in amusement as they argue absurdly and, in the end, the girl takes off her shoe.

"Both" says Cristina, pointing at her, "Smartass."

"What do you mean, both?" protests the girl.

"Do shoes and socks count as one garment, or do you leave the house with only one?"

"Cristina is right" Isabel intervenes, "we have to give this thing some excitement and if we use the shoes we won't finish all night."

"Votes in favor?" asks Luisa raising her hand.

All of them pick it up except the affected one, who, grimacing with annoyance, takes off her other shoe and returns. Isabel watches nervously as she throws the next one, because Marina is behind her and she is desperate to see how she is losing her clothes. Lucia, that's the name of the next one and she is Marta's cousin, who is also Isabel's best friend, throws the hoop with dexterity and misses by very little. She jumps happily because that gives her hope of making it on the next throw, so she also gets rid of her shoes and returns.

Now it's Marina's turn, who picks up the hoop from the ground and looks at it as if it were a meteorite just fallen from space. She stands behind the line and sighs.

"Come on, you can do it" Isabel encourages her behind her.

Marina positions herself, makes a couple of movements with her arm calculating the distance and finally throws the hoop and smashes it against the television. They all laugh, including her who, turning to Isabel with a totally involuntary gesture of complicity, takes off her sweater and throws it on the sofa. Isabel's eyes went to her waist when she did so, because the trajectory of the sweater caused the T-shirt she was wearing underneath to ride up a little and for a few moments left her belly uncovered. The sales clerk was fascinated by the sight and had to look away so as not to think about things she knew she shouldn't be thinking about.

"It's your turn" says Marina, who, instead of going back, stands next to her to see what she does.

Isabel takes the hoop that Cristina holds out to her and prepares to shoot. She, unlike probably all the others, is very calm. She has an excellent aim that she has never explained where it comes from. If only she had it with women too, she thinks, rolling her eyes. When she was a little girl, she used to compete in archery and also went with her father to practice skeet shooting whenever she could, leaving all those boastful men fascinated by her skill. Not wanting to appear overmatched from the start and not wanting the game to lose its excitement, she throws the hoop very low and sneaks it under the chair.

"Clothes" says Marina, demanding. She has been waiting for this moment since they started playing.

Isabel gives her a rather cocky look, takes off her shoes and they both return. In the next two rounds, only Lucia has managed to slip a hoop through a horn and Luisa has almost succeeded. Marina has just missed her third throw, she has already lost her sweater and booties and now she hesitates about the next garment. She looks at her socks and thinks about it, reminding the sales clerk of that time in the store when Marina couldn't decide on the tie. She thinks about it and it seems like a very distant memory, it is as if many things have happened since then that make her feel close to Marina, who continues to concentrate while she thinks about what to take off.

Isabel watches her with hawkish eyes, she knows that in a few more turns her new friend is going to have to take off more compromising garments, because in her opinion, throwing is the baddest of them all. Marina is about to take off her shirt because she knows that if she takes off her socks, her feet will freeze and that will make her uncomfortable, but, to Isabel's disgrace, at the last moment she remembers that she is wearing a belt in her pants and takes it off.

Isabel, disappointed because she has to keep waiting, gets mad as a child and decides that she is going to hit the next shot. And she hits it right on target, the hoop goes through the branch almost without grazing it.

"Ha!" she boasts cockily as if she had made a bet.

Marina follows her with her eyes when she returns. In her opinion, Isabel is a little crazy, but this point of madness is upsetting her. She really liked the ease with which she threw and hit that hoop that she is holding. Isabel has shown a very marked style that no doubt the others don't have, but that they haven't noticed in her friend, probably because none of them is looking at her as intensely as Marina is. She scratches the back of her neck a little uneasily and decides that she's not going to drink even one more sip of alcohol, she's sure that this increasingly strong attraction she feels towards Isabel, is the fault of that. It has to be.

Lucia has hit again, she has done it by pure chance, because Luisa has said something just when she was going to throw and has turned to her when she was releasing the hoop. Everyone applauds her luck except Isabel, because, besides having very good aim, she is tremendously competitive and only needs to be beaten by a fluke.

It is about to be Marina's turn and she is nervous, they are already at that point where it is time to show flesh and she feels a little self-conscious because she is the new one and she is sure that just because of that, she will be looked at more than the others. Luisa is already wearing pants and bra, another girl has preferred to keep the top garment and is showing her long legs around the dining room. None of them attracts Marina's attention because the only one she is eager to see in skimpy clothes is Isabel, and that makes her angry with herself. She knows that they are very different, that they collide like two freight trains as soon as one goes against the other, and the more that happens, the more interested she becomes. She nods and rubs her eyes in disbelief, she can't believe this is happening to her at her age. She pushes her hair away from her face and tucks it behind her ears because she is hot. Isabel looks at her slyly, she loves the permanent rosy color her new friend has been sporting on her cheeks for a while now. Marina discovers it and smiles at her automatically, she has not been able to contain herself, and it is just at that moment that Isabel wants to kiss her for the first time. Marina's heart bursts inside her chest, because she has sensed it, she has noticed that little concealed desire in Isabel's eyes and now her hands tremble and she feels a bubbling in her belly that she thought she would never feel again.

She turns around and turns her back to him, she is dazed and unfocused, although the latter does not worry her because she knows she will fail anyway. Isabel stands next to her as she has done every time, only now a tension has been unleashed between them that is very difficult for them to handle. They do not know how it happened, it is as if it had been there all the time, growing by leaps and bounds in silence, and it has been enough for them to cross each other's eyes for it to explode in their faces.

She is about to tell Isabel to move away, that her presence makes her very nervous, but she doesn't do it because that kind of nerves are not bad, they are adolescent nerves, those that settle in your body when you have the person you like next to you.

"Come on, Marina, don't think about it any longer" encourages Lucía, who is desperate to throw and see if she is still on a roll.

Marina throws the hoop without giving it much thought, it is the closest she has come to the horns and the only time it has simply fallen to the ground without hitting anything.

"Clothes, clothes, clothes..." they all shout as they have been doing the last few times.

Isabel doesn't, she just stares at her in such an intense way that Marina's blood rushes down to the same place. She pins her gaze on her as if all the others don't exist, and in a seductive and painfully slow way for Isabel, Marina removes her shirt and reveals herself to her in a lacy black bra that takes Isabel's breath away. She can't take her eyes off her no matter how hard she tries. She's sure she has a thousand flaws, but in her eyes, right now Marina is perfect and she finds her ravishingly sensual.

"It's your turn" Marina manages to vocalize, who, to her surprise, far from being uncomfortable with Isabel looking at her so shamelessly, likes it.

Isabel stands in front of her and Marina feels a desire, which she has a hard time containing, to press herself against her back and kiss her shoulder to wish her luck.

"I can't believe it" she mutters quietly to herself.

Isabel blinks a couple of times to shake her thoughts and focus, she is aware that whether she likes it or not, Marina is starting to like her a lot, but she also wants to win and for that she has to stop thinking about having her right behind her with her shirt off. She blinks again, frowns to fix her eyes and throws.

"Shit!" she shouts in obfuscation.

Isabel has failed and knows that Marina is entirely to blame. She takes off her sweater and throws it on the mountain of clothes overflowing on the sofa and returns to her seat with Marina. The first one eliminated falls in that round and Marina knows that she falls in the next one, because she only has her socks and pants left, and she has just taken them off after slamming the hoop against the leg of the chair. Isabel hasn't missed this time, and Marina's torso has her completely upset. Her head is filling up with more and more torrid thoughts and she wishes she wasn't so disgustingly competitive to take off some clothes too, because she feels she has too much to spare.

In the next round, Luisa, Cristina and three more girls fall. The only one who will still have clothes for one more throw is Lucia, because Marina, who is back behind the line with the hoop in her hand, knows that in this one she loses her pants and will have to wait in her underwear to see how the duel between Isabel and Lucia ends. She doesn't even bother to try to get close to the horns, she gets into position and throws the hoop, placing it on the books on a bookshelf.

"It's hard to do that" laughs Cristina from the sofa, infecting them all.

Marina turns to Isabel, who wipes away her smile as she undoes the button and pulls down the zipper. The next few seconds are torture for Isabel, she watches her undress and it seems like she is doing it for her. Marina is disconnected from everything else and when she finally takes off her pants, she hands them to Isabel as if they belong to her to the shocked looks of the others. Isabel swallows saliva, the garment still retains the warmth of Marina's body and she would like to keep it with her, like an amulet to give her luck she knows she doesn't need. Finally, she folds them with care and leaves them on the mountain. Now only she and Lucia are left, only that Lucia only has one more garment to take off while Isabel has three. The advantage is very clear and that reassures her, she knows that no matter how much her eyes go after Marina, she can't lose her concentration enough to fail three times, besides, Lucia's was pure luck.

Isabel shoots and hits the first time. She doesn't hold back the smile of satisfaction and Marina has to force it because now more than ever she wanted her to miss. She wants her clothes off. Lucia's turn comes, they all cheer and cheer for her, but it's no use, although she grazes the horn again, she misses and the hoop falls to the floor. Isabel jumps for joy as if she had won a millionaire prize and Lucia accepts her defeat with dignity and takes off the only garment she had left.

Luisa proposes a toast to celebrate how much fun they have had and makes them all swear that next year they will do it again.

Isabel and Marina accept her glass, but only take a sip because in both of their minds, alcohol is to blame for what is happening to them, even though they both know it's not true.

After the toast they all go to pick up their clothes, but discover to their horror that some of them have spilled their glass on them. Marina's pants are one of the most affected and she is very disgusted to put them on with that smell of cava.

"I'd lend you some, but because of you I haven't had time to stop by the house to get the suitcase" Isabel said, looking her up and down without hesitation.

"Because of me? You're the one who hit my car's ass" Marina defends herself.

"No, now it's my fault."

"Actually, you'd have a hard time proving that you're not the one who hit me from behind"

Isabel's jaw drops, that's something she didn't expect.

"I have the parking attendant as a witness, besides, you wouldn't dare lie" says Isabel, who doesn't know if Marina's cockiness pisses her off or excites her.

"Don't test me, and stop looking at me" asks Marina, shaking out her shirt to put it back on.

"I can't help it, I like you better with your clothes off."

Isabel's sincerity surprises Marina so much that she keeps her shirt in her hand without putting it on. Now her heart is pounding all over the place, Isabel is looking at her as if she wants to eat her, and she wants it with all her might.

"It's not fair that you can see me without clothes and I can't see you."

Now Isabel is the one who looks at her dumbfounded, she did not expect Marina to be so direct.

"I don't like injustice" Isabel takes Marina by the hand and leads her down the hallway to her room.

When they enter, she closes the door and before Marina can say anything or have a chance to run away, Isabel begins to take off her clothes to the rhythm of the music playing in the background in the dining room. Marina thinks it is the most erotic thing she has ever seen in her life, and Isabel is not a very good dancer.

"Now we're the same way" she says when she gets down to her underwear. She's so nervous it's hard to breathe.

If a few hours ago she had been told that she and the woman she almost strangled with a tie were going to be half naked in her room, she would have had a fit of giggles. To her surprise, Marina takes the initiative by approaching her and cornering her against the wall with her body.

"Are you sure you want to do this?" she asks very close to her lips.

Isabel responds by wrapping her hands around Marina's waist, pulling her in until her pubis brushes against hers and they both begin to tremble with excitement. When Marina places her hands on Isabel's cheeks and kisses her, everything disappears around them both, the music stops playing, the screams and laughter of the other women become a distant echo and there is only space left for them. The two of them fall on the bed already completely naked and look at each other panting, ready to let their bodies do the talking and release all the tension that exists between them.

Chapter 9

Marina is woken up by a vibration of her cell phone on the bedside table. She opens her eyes and sees some light in the room, it is very dim and comes from under the door, it seems that someone left the hallway light on, because the house is completely silent, except for the soft snoring of Isabel, who sleeps soundly next to her. Marina watches her in the semi-darkness and remembers with absolute clarity everything that happened last night in that bed. She feels a jolt of excitement between her legs and swallows saliva scared of herself.

She doesn't understand what is happening to her with Isabel, she was sure that, when she woke up, more rested and serene, she would regret having let herself go like that, but she doesn't. There is nothing about what she did last night that makes her feel bad, nor is there anything about Isabel that causes her to want to run away. Still, she decides she's leaving. Because Marina hadn't planned for this, there are things in her that had lain dormant for a long time and this awakening has her bewildered and frightened. She looks at Isabel once more and feels the temptation to pull her hair away from her neck and kiss her in that area, that still scares her more. She turns around with bated breath and looks at her cell phone, the message is from her brother asking her if she is okay. Last night she forgot to tell him she was staying over, but how could she not forget if she hadn't planned to, and once they walked through the bedroom door she couldn't think of anything but Isabel. He tells her he's fine so she can rest easy. It is half past seven in the morning and she knows that he must have been awake for a while with the children, who must have gotten up in search of the presents their parents had left them, because she had already given them theirs, claiming that Santa Claus had passed by their house earlier.

She takes one last look at Isabel and gets out of bed with a feeling of guilt for leaving like that, but she consoles herself with the thought that, if they have to talk about this, they can do it when they meet to fill out the accident report. While she searches for her underwear on the floor, also using the light of her cell phone, Marina thinks about whether she should at least leave her a note. Right now she is a sea of doubts, everything scares her and she doesn't know how to act, and to that she must add that she doesn't know what Isabel thinks, surely for her it was a one night stand, a reward for the disastrous afternoon she had given her. She puts on her underwear and T-shirt, which is the only thing she brought into the room, and stealthily exits the room. When she reaches the dining room, the couch has been converted into a bed and there are three women sleeping on it on one leg. She assumes that the third is the one who was supposed to share a room and bed with Isabel, but she took that place without permission. Suddenly she feels like an intruder and searches desperately for her clothes. She finds her pants on a chair and a single sock next to her booties. She dresses as quickly as she can, grabs her coat and purse and leaves the house.

When she goes outside, she's grateful for the cold blow she gets. She calculates that it must be two or three degrees, but at least it's not snowing. She ties up her hair as best she can so as not to look crazy because she hasn't even been to the bathroom and doesn't know what she looks like. As she enters her house, everyone turns to her, including the children who yell at her to come see their toys.

"I'll take a shower real quick and come downstairs, honey" she assures the youngest.

And Marina runs upstairs to her room while the amused eyes of her brother and sister-in-law follow her until she disappears. The shower has cleared her mind, but it doesn't take away the uneasy feeling she feels for not having said goodbye to Isabel. When she goes downstairs, she plays for a while with her nephews and nieces to avoid any questions from her brother or sister-in-law and, after a time that seems understandable to her, she announces that she is leaving.

"So soon? But you don't go back to work until day two" protests her sister-in-law.

"I know, but I want to take the opportunity to do some things at home, and I also have to meet Lola if I don't want her to stop talking to me" she deliberately exaggerates.

"What about your other friend? The one here, aren't you going to meet her again?" asks her brother with full intention.

"Yes, maybe I'll see her" she answers stifled, "she also lives in the city, anyway, I'm leaving before the snow starts to fall"

When Isabel wakes up she stays very still in her place because she doesn't want to wake Marina. Her heart begins to pound as her treacherous mind starts to remember very realistically everything that happened last night. She never imagined that Marina was so fiery in bed, she remembers how she snorted as she held in her moans because she was embarrassed for the others to hear her and her heart starts to race a little faster.

She is surprised by the fervent desire to repeat it again, this time in a more intimate place because she does not want Marina to hold back. She sighs slowly trying to relax the frenetic rhythm of her vital organ and turns to her to contemplate her silhouette in the half-light, and it is then when she discovers with disgust that Marina is no longer by her side. Isabel flicks on the light because she needs to make sure. She can't describe how it feels to see that Marina has really left, how long ago? She feels with her hand the place where she should have been and finds it cold. She gets up abruptly and walks around the bed to check if she has left a note on the bedside table, she finds nothing and that gives her a feeling of emptiness that she doesn't like and can't understand either.

She has just gotten angry with herself, she tells herself that it was only one night, that she has done it before and the next day she was happy if her lovers did not wake up next to her, she even wished it when they did. Why then doesn't the same thing happen to her now? She runs to her cell phone thinking that maybe she has left her a message there, but among the many she has wishing her a Merry Christmas, there is none from Marina.

"Bitch" she spits under her breath with a mixture of anger and disappointment.

"What did I expect?" Marina and her are completely different, a few hours ago she couldn't stand her and wished she had never met her, what has changed? She steals some clean panties from her friend Marta, who is the one she should have shared the room with, gathers the rest of her clothes and leaves the room to one of the two bathrooms in the house. She takes a shower that removes any trace of Marina's smell on her skin, but not her memories, because every time she closes her eyes she sees her naked on that bed and she can remember that sweet almond smell that her skin gave off as if she had her in front again.

When she leaves the bathroom and enters the dining room, Marta and Cristina are already up and have prepared coffee and toast for everyone.

"Here is the winner of the night" says Cristina smiling when she sees her.

"Good morning" she greets in a curt tone.

"Marina hasn't gotten up yet?" asks her friend Marta cautiously, since she knows Isabel too well and knows from the tense expression on her face that something is not right.

"Marina has left."

"When?" Cristina, who was sleeping in the dining room and hadn't seen her leave, was surprised.

"No idea, I didn't hear."

"Neither do we" adds Marta.

"Hasn't she said goodbye to you?" asks Cristina, earning a nudge from Marta.

"No. I'm not saying it woke me up, but I don't know, a message would have been nice" she complains, pouring coffee into a cup.

"Maybe something came up, Isabel" said Marta, who had never seen her so angry about something like this, trying to calm her down, "I'm sure she'll call you later"

"Yeah, sure."

Isabel sits with them and sips her coffee while she angrily thinks that she is going to have to be the one to call Marina, because her car is still in the parking lot with a wrecked front end and if they don't fill out the accident report she will have to pay for it out of her own pocket, and that is something she has no intention of doing.

"I'm going home" she announces after washing her cup.

"What? Why?" Marta wants to know" we still have one more night here, Isabel, don't be a spoilsport."

"I'll stain the mood if I stay, believe me, I've slept very little and..."

"We know that" Cristina interrupts her, amused.

"I think I need to sleep the rest of the day to be a person. We'll meet up when you get back to the city."

"All right" Marta agrees, "take my car and leave it parked in front of my house, I'll go back to the city with Lucía."

"Thank you" says Isabel accepting the keys from her friend, she knows that a cab will cost her an arm and a leg and she is not willing to show up at Marina's family home to ask her for a ride.

Chapter 10

Isabel has tried to do what she told her friends. She spent her time until lunchtime, lying on the couch watching Christmas movies like the Grinch or Santa Claus! She preferred childish things to anything that had a romantic story and reminded her of Marina. She must admit with disappointment that she has not been very successful because, although she managed to distract herself on many occasions, she has checked her cell phone more times than she would like to see if Marina had decided to say something to her.

When she finishes eating, she huffs and decides it is best to settle the matter as soon as possible. It's clear that Marina has run away from her and she doesn't blame her, they didn't start off on the right foot and she made some unfortunate comments, but what was she going to do? Because of that woman she was locked in the store and then almost lost her car.

Marina is at home, sitting on the sofa in her pajamas, reluctantly flipping through channels when her cell phone starts to ring. She has not yet looked at the screen to see who it is and her heart has already skipped a beat at the thought of Isabel. She knows she has not acted well this morning, she could have had the detail to tell her something, at least inform her that she was leaving town or make it clear how much fun she had last night, but she has not done it no matter how tempted she feels at all times. The panic of a rebuff from Isabel doesn't let her react. That woman is a ticking time bomb and Marina finds it hard to adapt to things she can't control or foresee. She told her friend

Lola everything when they spoke half an hour ago and explained everything that happened yesterday with Isabel, from beginning to end.

"Let me get this straight, yesterday you got locked in a store with a sales clerk who, by chance, you hit with your car at the exit of a parking lot?"

"Marina interrupted her, still thinking that if Isabel had not been anxious and had kept a prudent distance, it would not have happened."

"I don't care whose fault it was" Lola grumbled, "and don't cut me off again. You met her again, and if that wasn't enough, she happened to be going to the same town as you. You drive off together and then she invites you to have a drink at her house with her friends. It turns out that the girl is not as much of a dick as you thought and you end up in bed fucking like rabbits..."

"I didn't say rabbits" Marina interrupted her again, overwhelmed by her friend's foul language.

"Shut up" cried Lola indignantly, "don't you realize it's fate? It has made you stumble over and over again until the sparks have jumped, and then you grab it and run away."

"I didn't run away..."

"No? And what do you call what you have done?"

Marina didn't know how to respond to that. She knows her friend is right. She likes Isabel, she is the first woman who has awakened her interest after Elisa. She doesn't know what she sees in her, she's a woman of the bunch, with a lot of character and quite rude and disconcerting. Maybe it's those eyes between amber and brown that keep bewitching Marina every time she looks at her, or that way of smiling at her in a sincere way when they don't argue, it could also be the confidence with which

Isabel speaks to her or that edge she uses when she gets angry that Marina finds charming.

The cell phone rings again and she realizes that she has been absorbed in her thoughts and has not answered the previous call. She stretches like a cat to reach it and when she looks at the screen her worst fears come true and the air escapes from her lungs. Seeing Isabel's name on the screen makes her so nervous that she has to concentrate so as not to get the wrong icon and reject the call instead of answering it as has happened to her on occasion. Finally, she places her thumb on the accept icon and slides it to the right.

"Hello, Isabel" she says, she is red with embarrassment as she clears her throat.

"Hi. Is it okay if we meet this afternoon for a moment? I need to get the car settled as soon as possible."

Isabel has been polite and direct, something that does not surprise Marina because that woman is like that, she has no filter and does not know how to dissimulate. Marina realizes at that moment how authentic Isabel is and that makes her smile like a fool.

"Yes, of course. Where do you want to meet?" she asks with her heart racing.

"In front of the parking lot there is a cafeteria, we can meet there."

Isabel continues with that dry tone that makes Marina uncomfortable. The tension has returned between them as in almost every moment they have spent together. She knows that she should mention that cowardly escape of hers this morning, but then she thinks that maybe Isabel is not being so rude because of that, maybe it's because she regrets what happened last night between them and what she needs is to solve the car issue as soon as possible so she doesn't have to see her again. That makes her tense and causes a pang of anguish in the pit of her stomach.

"All right, I'll see you there in an hour" says Marina, who suddenly feels like hanging up.

Marina gets up from the sofa, obfuscated. The idea of meeting Isabel again has made her very nervous. Now she doesn't know what to wear, she feels the need to dress up for her, to show herself as beautiful as she can so that Isabel recovers the desire she felt for her last night, or maybe she was just horny and took advantage of the fact that she was available? It is said that it can't be that, she saw how Isabel was looking at her and remembers very well that phrase she whispered to him when she was still in her underwear: *I like you better without clothes*. She was sincere when she said it, because Isabel is that direct, she doesn't bite her tongue or keep anything to herself, sometimes which can be offensive, and sometimes charming as it seemed to Marina last night. She's been thinking about that phrase all day, because if she likes it better without clothes it's because she also likes it with clothes on, right?

She sighs and rubs her temples hard to relax a little. Whether she likes it or not, she's going to meet her again, so she dresses as she always does because she's decided she doesn't want to sell Isabel something she's not.

When she arrives at the cafeteria, it doesn't take her long to locate Isabel, even though it is full of people. She is the only woman sitting alone at a table in the middle of the room. Marina would have liked a place a little more discreet and less crowded, but she understands that since it is Christmas, Isabel was lucky to find a free table.

Isabel fixes her eyes on Marina as soon as she sees her walk through the door. Her pulse quickens and she feels her heart pounding in the center of her chest. That bothers her, she is angry and does not want to feel everything she feels, she wants by her side a determined woman who is not afraid to call things by their name or face problems head on. Marina doesn't fit that profile, now they are looking at each other and she perceives that indecision in her eyes, the same she had when she was looking at the ties on their noses. She sees her swallowing saliva with effort and finally, starts walking towards her. Isabel stands up out of politeness and the two of them stand facing each other like two indecisive girls, although Isabel is clear that if things had been otherwise, she would greet her right now with a kiss on the lips, because that's what she feels like doing, She feels a growing and overwhelming need to kiss her again, but she cannot do it because it is clear that Marina does not feel the same way she does, otherwise she would not have run away this morning the way she did, or at least she would have called her afterwards, but she has not pronounced herself and that has Isabel in a constant state of alert.

Marina trembles from top to bottom and she doesn't know why. Isabel's gaze is piercing her and she feels a flutter growing in her chest that makes it difficult for her to breathe or think clearly. She knows she can't stand there like a fool for long, she is the one who has arrived last, and it is up to her to take the step of greeting Isabel who, to complicate things even more, has risen from her chair. What does she do now? Does she kiss her twice? Does she shake her hand? Or does she kiss her on the lips and ask her to go home as she is eager to do?

"Are you going to say something, or are you just going to stand there like a stunned stare?" Isabel lets go, bringing her back to the real world.

The fact that she is so rude doesn't help her at all, but even so, she plucks up her courage and approaches her to give her two kisses. Isabel practically doesn't move and returns them in a very superficial way, which hurts Marina a lot, but she doesn't say anything and they both sit down.

"I brought a report I had at home" says Marina in one breath.

She has opened her bag and shakes the inside nervously. Isabel's cold reaction continues to make an incomprehensible impression on her, a lump has formed in her throat and she feels like crying. Now she feels stupid for thinking that maybe something more could happen between them, but it's clear that Isabel doesn't feel the same way.

She finds the report and places it on the table. Isabel has taken out a pen and has begun to draw the sketch of the two cars while Marina asks the waiter for an infusion. Playing for time until the waiter brings it to her, Marina watches Isabel as she finishes the sketch and fills in her side with her data. She likes the look of concentration on her face and the elegant way she holds her pen. She also notices her fingers, her manicured nails or the almost imperceptible freckles on her nose that give her a mischievous air that is very much in keeping with Isabel's character.

The infusion appears in front of her, startling her just as Isabel finishes filling in her data.

"If you agree, fill in your side and we're done" says Isabel, dragging the part towards Marina.

Her knot grows uncontrollably. Marina hardly notices the drawing, she only knows that she is the guilty party and accepts it without reneging because it was really like that, maybe Isabel did not keep her distance, but the fact is that the car went backwards and if her lover's car had not been there to stop her, maybe she would have ended up embedded in a column.

Isabel notices that Marina is holding the pen very tightly because her hand is shaking. Her handwriting is a bit irregular and she makes a couple of scratches. She suddenly feels bad for the coldness with which she is treating her, she knows her very little, but Marina is very transparent and Isabel realizes that she is very nervous and in complete tension. She has noticed her white knuckles or how her other hand crushes the paper firmly on the table. Now she would like to take that free hand, caress it and try to convey calmness, but she refuses to do so, of the two, the one who is clearly hesitating with everything is Marina, and Isabel, although she feels bad, does not want to make things easy for him. If she really wants to talk about what happened last night, she is not going to be the one to bring up the subject, she needs Marina to be the one to take the first step and show decision for once.

"I think that's it, check it if you want to" says Marina, handing back the report.

Isabel examines her with a clinical eye, not because she doesn't trust Marina, but because she is trying to give her time to calm down.

"I think it's all there."

"Okay" Marina answers without looking at her.

Now they are already in that tense moment that often involves them.

"Are you leaving already?" asks Marina in an outburst when Isabel picks up her bag to put the report away.

"Unless you want to tell me something, I don't think I have a role to play here. Do you want to tell me something, Marina?" she asks inquisitively.

"You mean last night?"

Isabel is extremely glad that Marina made reference to that, but it also makes her angry to see the panic in the expression in her eyes.

"I don't mean anything" she replies curtly without looking away from her.

"Maybe we could talk about it" says Marina, who is becoming more and more tense.

She feels like an imbecile, because she has a clear opportunity to know what Isabel thinks about it and she doesn't know how to express to her what she felt last night or what she feels now, which is nothing more than a crazy desire for Isabel to give her a simple hug. That's all she needs and she knows she'll calm down. Then she could walk her to the parking lot and keep her company while the tow truck comes, and then invite her to her house for privacy and a quiet talk about it. But she knows that Isabel is not going to give her that hug if she doesn't ask for it, it has become clear to her that this woman is not going to lift a finger if she doesn't do it first, and Marina is very indecisive.

"It's been a pleasure, Marina, look for me when you know what you want."

Marina feels like she is about to spit her own heart out of her mouth when she sees Isabel walking towards the door. She shivers and feels her strength failing her. She should yell at her to wait for her or run after her, but Isabel is quick and has quickly disappeared from sight. She raises her hand to ask the waiter for the bill and, while she takes it with a parsimony that seems desperate, Marina can't stop thinking about Isabel's last sentence:" Look for me when you know what you want." What did she mean? The answer will come when she is already at home and calls her friend Lola to tell her what has happened, after having gone to the parking lot and not having found Isabel.

"That you're an asshole, that's what she meant. She's put it on a plate for you, Marina, and you always have your damn doubts. Do you like that woman?" asks her friend in a demanding tone.

"Yes, I do like her" she says, surprised.

"Well, you know what you have to do."

Chapter 11

Marina knows what she has to do and yet she has done nothing. Two days have passed and she hasn't lifted a finger. She has let the fear of Isabel's reaction or rejection dominate her, but today she has woken up with a different mentality. She is fed up with her fears and indecision and is aware that things are not going to be easy for her, if she wants something with Isabel, she is going to have to fight for it.

She takes a shower and takes her time, she doesn't want to get nervous, she has made a decision and intends to accept any answer from Isabel with dignity, after all, she is an adult woman and not a child, she should behave as such. When she gets out of the shower, she dries her hair and gets ready the same way she always does, but this time she sprays a few drops of her favorite perfume, the one she only wears on special occasions.

Marina arrives at the same street where three days ago she walked desperate to find the last gift she was missing. This time it's not snowing, but it's a little breezy and, besides, the temperatures have dropped and the coat is not enough to protect her from the coldness of the air.

It's almost the same time she entered Isabel's store the other day, it's only ten minutes to closing time. Marina observes the Christmas lights on the street and listens to the songs playing over the loudspeakers, recovering a part of the childhood illusion that those dates used to give her, and then she arrives at the door of Isabel's store and, without a second's hesitation, she enters.

Isabel is hanging several pants on their respective hangers when she hears the bell at the door. She snorts and looks at the clock reluctantly, another last minute customer and she is alone in the store again. She walks out grumbling to herself and cursing her bad luck, until she looks up and finds Marina standing in front of the counter. She doesn't know what's happening to her body at that moment, she's been in a bad mood for two days debating whether she should be the one to finally, finally take a step towards Marina if she wants something with her, because it's clear that she's too much of a coward to do anything. And now she's there.

"Do you want something?" asks Isabel, unable to contain her inner rage.

"You" Marina disarmed her.

"What?" Isabel hesitates for the first time.

"You said to look for you when I know what I want, didn't you?"

"Yeah" Isabel stammers, feeling stupid. It is the first time she is speechless, so the situation is new to her and she does not know how to deal with it.

Marina shows an unfamiliar confidence on the other side of the counter. She looks at her calmly and that gleam in her eyes, which disturbs Isabel so much, has doubled in intensity.

"I know what I want, I want to invite you to dinner if you don't have plans for tonight. And if you do, invite you tomorrow, or the next day, I don't take no for an answer."

Isabel looks at her in amazement at her determination, suddenly, all her anger has vanished and she only wishes the remaining minutes would pass before she closes and leaves with Marina. A man approaches to pay for some pants, Marina steps aside while Isabel charges him, but she doesn't stop looking at her. Isabel smiles absurdly, she can't help it and is only afraid that the man in front of her won't get confused and think that he is the one who snatches that sudden happiness from her. When the man leaves, Isabel looks at the clock again and goes out behind her to pull down the shutter and prevent more people from entering and lengthening her stay in there.

"There's something else I want" says Marina when Isabel comes back behind the counter.

"What is it?" she asks confused.

"Pay for the tie."

Isabel didn't even remember that, but Marina has already pulled out her purse and holds out her credit card.

"It's not necessary, Marina, consider it a payment for having taken me to the village that night."

"It's not negotiable, Isabel" Marina insists without taking her hand away.

Isabel smiles again, she loves this new version of Marina so determined and doesn't want to take it away from her with one of her hateful replies.

"As you wish."

They make the payment and Isabel begins to collect everything.

"If you wait a couple of minutes, we'll have dinner tonight" she asks nervously.

"I'll wait for you for as long as it takes" says Marina calmly.

This time it is Isabel who feels the trembling in her legs and who has to concentrate so as not to make a mistake with the things she has to do. When she finally closes the register and has everything, she walks to the other side of the counter with her purse in her hand and her heart pounding.

"I think we can go now" she announces quickly.

When she gets closer to her, Marina is once again hypnotized by Isabel's eyes, she still doesn't know what her exact color is and she doesn't care, because that's Isabel, an unpredictable woman.

"What?" asks Isabel with a nervous smile when she sees that Marina keeps looking at her.

But Marina doesn't have time to answer because the lights suddenly go out.

"It can't be" Isabel mumbles incredulously, "you're a jinx" she spits without thinking in the gloom. They are locked up again.

Marina is not bothered by the accusation this time; on the contrary, it makes her smile and search for Isabel's body in the dim light provided by the emergency lights. When she finds her, invites her to sit on the counter and she settles between her legs.

"I can think of a more entertaining way to wait for the light to come back on" she whispers, pressing herself against her.

Isabel thinks the idea is so good that she doesn't discuss it, she simply moistens her lips and kisses Marina as she has been wanting to do for days.

END